TALES FROM
FAZBEAR'S

This is a work of fiction. Similarities to real people, places, or events are entirely coincidental.

TALES FROM FAZBEAR'S

First edition. July 16, 2024.

Copyright © 2024 Farkas Döme.

ISBN: 979-8227455390

Written by Farkas Döme.

AUTHOR BIOGRAPHY

Greetings, I'm Döme, a devoted student whose universe orbits around the mesmerizing mysteries of Five Nights at Freddy's. The eerie ambiance and intricate storytelling of Freddy Fazbear's Pizza have ensnared my imagination like nothing else. As an ardent fan of the series, I am endlessly intrigued by unraveling the secrets of the animatronics and delving deep into its haunting lore.

Beyond my fandom, I am an enthusiastic writer. Writing serves as my creative outlet, allowing me to craft suspenseful narratives inspired by the enigmatic characters of FNaF or venture into entirely new worlds and genres. It's not merely a pastime; it's a profound passion that enables me to bring to life the thrilling experiences and eerie atmospheres that I adore about FNaF.

Balancing my academic pursuits with my love for storytelling is a rewarding challenge. When not immersed in studies, you'll often find me at my desk, surrounded by scribbled plot ideas, sketched character arcs, and stacks of FNaF lore books for inspiration. Each story I write is a voyage of exploration and revelation, where I strive to capture the suspense and intrigue that captivate me within the games.

In my world, academia and creativity converge, fueling a perpetual quest for knowledge and growth as both a student and a writer. The meticulous research and critical thinking demanded by my studies complement my imaginative endeavors, enriching my storytelling with depth and authenticity.

Through my writing, I invite readers to embark on journeys through the shadows and secrets of my imagination. Whether exploring the sinister mysteries of Freddy Fazbear's Pizza or charting new territories of suspense and horror, each twist and turn promises new excitement and deeper mysteries to uncover.

EPIGRAPH

"Sometimes the most unlikely friendships are the ones that transform us the most, bridging gaps we never knew existed."

FOREWORD

Welcome to a delightful collection of tales from the heart of Freddy Fazbear's Pizza! In this book, you'll find a series of whimsical, humorous stories that capture the charm and joy of the Afton family and their beloved pizzeria, all before the darker days came to pass.

Imagine a place where laughter never ends and every day is a new adventure. Freddy Fazbear's Pizza was more than just a restaurant—it was a magical world where animatronics sang, danced, and brought endless smiles to children and adults alike. At the center of this joyful universe was the Afton family, always ready to bring a bit of extra magic to every moment.

These stories are not bound by the lore you might know but are instead inspired by the spirit of fun and creativity that Freddy Fazbear's Pizza embodies. From hilarious mishaps with the animatronics to heartwarming family moments, each tale in this collection is crafted to entertain and bring a smile to your face.

Join us as we step into a world where William Afton is more likely to be found tweaking a malfunctioning animatronic for comedic effect rather than sinister purposes, and where every family dinner at Freddy Fazbear's is an event to remember. These stories celebrate the lighter side of the Five Nights at Freddy's universe, inviting you to enjoy a good laugh and perhaps even a bit of nostalgia for the carefree days of childhood.

Whether you're a longtime fan or new to the world of Freddy Fazbear's, this collection is sure to tickle your funny bone and warm your heart. So, sit back, relax, and get ready for a series of adventures that highlight the joy, humor, and quirky moments that made Freddy Fazbear's Pizza a place of endless fun.

Welcome to the funny side of Freddy Fazbear's Pizza!

ACKNOWLEDGEMENTS

First and foremost, I want to express my deepest gratitude to all the fans of the Five Nights at Freddy's universe. Your passion and creativity have inspired this collection of stories, and your unwavering support has made this project possible.

A special thank you goes to Scott Cawthon, the brilliant mind behind Five Nights at Freddy's. Your creation has not only provided endless entertainment but has also sparked the imaginations of countless fans around the world. This book is a testament to the world you've built and the joy it continues to bring.

To my family and friends, thank you for your endless encouragement and for believing in this project from the very beginning. Your patience and understanding have been invaluable, especially during the late nights and long hours spent writing.

To the beta readers and early supporters, your feedback and enthusiasm have been crucial in refining these stories. Your constructive critiques and positive comments have helped make this book the best it can be.

Lastly, to the readers—new and old—thank you for picking up this book and diving into the world of Freddy Fazbear's Pizza with me. I hope these stories bring a smile to your face and a bit of joy to your day. Your support means the world to me, and I can't wait to share more adventures with you in the future.

With heartfelt thanks,

Döme

INTRODUCTION

Welcome to the enchanting and whimsical world of Freddy Fazbear's Pizza, where every corner holds a tale waiting to be told, and every character is brimming with personality and charm. This book is a collection of light-hearted and humorous stories that take you behind the scenes of the iconic pizzeria, focusing on the fun and quirky adventures of the Afton family and their lovable animatronic friends.

In these pages, you won't find the dark and mysterious lore that often surrounds the Five Nights at Freddy's universe. Instead, we've set our sights on the joy, laughter, and everyday mishaps that make Freddy Fazbear's Pizza a place of endless entertainment and delight. Think of this book as a playful peek into a world where the animatronics' biggest challenges are more likely to be spontaneous dance-offs than sinister schemes.

You'll get to know William Afton, not as the enigmatic figure of darker tales, but as a creative inventor with a knack for getting into amusing predicaments. His family, full of vibrant personalities, adds to the mix, creating a lively and dynamic backdrop for these stories. From animatronics that just can't seem to get their routines right to heartwarming moments of family togetherness, each story is designed to bring a smile to your face and a laugh to your heart.

This collection is for everyone who has ever been captivated by the magic of Freddy Fazbear's Pizza, whether you're a long-time fan or someone discovering it for the first time. It's a tribute to the lighter side of the Five Nights at Freddy's universe, where the focus is on fun, friendship, and the joy of making memories.

So grab a slice of pizza, settle in, and get ready to join the Afton family and their animatronic companions on a series of delightful adventures. Welcome to a place where every day is a celebration, and every story is a reminder that even in a world known for its mysteries, there's always room for a little laughter.

Enjoy the stories!

A NEW BEGINNING: SPRING BONNIE and CASSIDY

Spring Bonnie and Cassidy's friendship stood as a testament to the magic that can happen when we look beyond appearances and take the time to understand one another. In a world filled with animatronics and secrets, they found a connection that defied the odds, proving that friendship can be found in the most unexpected places.

found a connection that defied the odds, proving that friendship can be found in the most unexpected places.Cassidy was a curious boy, his bright blonde hair always tousled from his adventures. The local pizzeria, Freddy Fazbear's Pizza, was his favorite place to explore. The animatronics fascinated him, especially Spring Bonnie, who always seemed different from the rest.

One sunny afternoon, while other kids played games and enjoyed pizza, Cassidy noticed something peculiar. Spring Bonnie, usually lively and entertaining, was sitting quietly on the stage, eyes dimmed. Intrigued, Cassidy approached the animatronic.

"Hey, Spring Bonnie," Cassidy said softly, unsure if he would get a response.

To his surprise, Spring Bonnie's eyes flickered, and he turned to face Cassidy. "Hello there," the animatronic replied in a gentle, almost hesitant voice.

Cassidy's eyes widened in amazement. "You can talk?"

Spring Bonnie nodded. "Yes, but I usually don't. People don't notice when I do."

Cassidy sat down on the stage, legs dangling over the edge. "Why not? I think it's cool that you can talk."

Spring Bonnie's expression softened. "Most kids are scared of us, but you seem different."

"I'm not scared," Cassidy said confidently. "I think you're awesome."

Spring Bonnie's mechanical face attempted a smile. "Thank you. It's been a long time since anyone wanted to talk to me."

Cassidy grinned. "Well, I'm here now. We can be friends."

Days turned into weeks, and Cassidy visited the pizzeria every chance he got. He and Spring Bonnie shared stories, played games, and even created secret hand signals for fun. Cassidy learned that Spring Bonnie had a playful spirit, always coming up with new games and jokes to keep their time together exciting.

One day, Cassidy brought a sketchpad and some pencils. "I thought we could draw together," he suggested.

Spring Bonnie tilted his head curiously. "I've never tried drawing before."

Cassidy laughed. "There's a first time for everything! Here, I'll show you."

They spent hours sketching various things – other animatronics, funny faces, and even a self-portrait of Spring Bonnie. Cassidy's laughter filled the room as Spring Bonnie attempted to draw with his large, mechanical hands.

"You're pretty good at this!" Cassidy encouraged.

Spring Bonnie chuckled. "Thanks to you."

As their friendship grew, Spring Bonnie revealed more about himself. "I wasn't always like this," he confided one evening. "There was a time when I was just like you, a kid who loved to play."

Cassidy's eyes widened in curiosity. "What happened?"

Spring Bonnie's eyes dimmed slightly. "It's a long story, one that involves a lot of sadness. But meeting you has made things better."

Cassidy reached out and placed a hand on Spring Bonnie's metal arm. "You're not alone anymore. We'll face everything together."

Their bond became stronger with each passing day. Cassidy's presence brought a warmth to Spring Bonnie's mechanical heart, a reminder of the joy and innocence he once knew. And in return, Spring

Bonnie gave Cassidy a friendship unlike any other, one filled with adventure, laughter, and unwavering support.

Years later, Cassidy would look back on those days with fondness. The pizzeria had changed, but the memories of his time with Spring Bonnie remained etched in his heart. He knew that no matter where life took him, the friendship he forged with an animatronic bunny would always be a cherished part of his story.

A DAY AT THE BEACH WITH THE AFTONS

The Afton family rarely ventured beyond the imposing walls of their Victorian mansion, but on this particular summer day, they found themselves drawn to the allure of the beach. William Afton, a man of stoic demeanor and sharp intellect, had reluctantly agreed to Clara's gentle insistence that they spend a day away from the shadows that haunted their estate.

Clara Afton, her gentle demeanor a stark contrast to her husband's sternness, had packed a picnic basket filled with delicacies—crustless sandwiches, fresh fruit, and chilled lemonade. Her eyes sparkled with excitement as she watched their children, Michael and Evan, eagerly explore the sandy shore.

Michael, the elder of the two boys, had inherited his father's brooding intensity and insatiable curiosity. He strode along the water's edge, his dark hair tousled by the sea breeze, collecting shells and driftwood with a keen eye for detail.

Evan, the younger son, trailed behind him with a grin that could rival the sun itself. His blonde hair gleamed in the sunlight, his laughter echoing across the beach as he chased seagulls and dug for buried treasure in the sand.

As the day unfolded, the Afton family settled into a rhythm of laughter and relaxation that seemed to wash away the weight of their responsibilities. William, normally consumed by thoughts of his work and the mysteries that lurked within their mansion, found himself drawn into a spirited game of beach volleyball with his sons. Clara, her worries momentarily forgotten, joined them with a grace that belied her years.

Picnic blankets were spread beneath the shade of a lone palm tree, its fronds whispering secrets in the gentle breeze. The Aftons shared stories and laughter as they savored Clara's homemade treats, the taste of freedom mingling with the salt of the sea air.

Evan built sandcastles with Cassidy, his best friend from school who had joined them for the day. Cassidy's laughter blended seamlessly with Evan's as they constructed elaborate fortresses adorned with seashells and seaweed, their imaginations transforming the beach into a realm of fantasy and adventure.

Meanwhile, Michael wandered further down the shore, his mind wandering with the ebb and flow of the tide. He discovered a hidden cove where tide pools teemed with life—colorful fish darting through crystal-clear waters and starfish clinging to rocky crevices.

As the sun began its descent towards the horizon, casting hues of gold and pink across the sky, the Afton family gathered once more on the beach. They watched in awe as seagulls wheeled overhead and waves crashed against the shore, a symphony of nature's beauty that mirrored the harmony within their own hearts.

In that fleeting moment, amidst the sand and surf, the Afton family found a sense of peace and unity that had eluded them within the confines of their mansion. They held onto the memory of that day—the laughter, the joy, and the bond that strengthened with each shared smile—as they returned to the shadows of their estate, carrying with them the promise of more days like this to come.

On that sun-kissed beach, the Afton family discovered that even amidst their secrets and shadows, moments of joy and togetherness could illuminate their lives like the brightest of stars in the night sky.

A DAY AT FREADBEAR'S FAMILY DINER

In the heart of a cozy town surrounded by rolling hills and picturesque meadows, stood Fredbear's Family Diner – a cherished haven of joy and wonderment for children and families alike. The diner, adorned with bright colors and whimsical decorations, radiated a warm invitation to all who passed by.William Afton and Henry Emily, lifelong friends and business partners of Fredbear's Family Diner, received a special invitation from their own establishment. The invitation, playfully designed with Fredbear and Spring Bonnie, promised a day of festivities and celebration for their families.

"Henry, my old friend, I believe our little diner has outdone itself this time!" William exclaimed with a hearty laugh, reading over the invitation.

Henry nodded with a grin. "Indeed, William. I'm looking forward to seeing the children's faces light up today. Let's make it a day to remember."

The families gathered their excitement and set out for Fredbear's, eager to immerse themselves in the magic of the diner they lovingly owned and operated together.As the Afton and Emily families arrived at Fredbear's, they were greeted by the familiar sight of Fredbear and Spring Bonnie – the beloved animatronics who stood as guardians of fun and joy at the entrance. The children squealed with delight, rushing to hug their larger-than-life friends.

"Welcome, welcome!" William and Henry chimed in unison, their voices brimming with enthusiasm as they embraced their families and welcomed them inside.

The interior of Fredbear's was a bustling hub of activity and color. Arcade machines blinked invitingly, a carousel of laughter spun children round and round, and the sweet aroma of freshly baked treats wafted from the kitchen. William and Henry exchanged proud glances as they watched their vision come to life.The day unfolded with a myriad of activities designed to delight guests of all ages. William and Henry joined their children – Michael, Elizabeth, and Evan for the Aftons, and Sammy and Charlie for the Emilys – in exploring every corner of the diner.

They started at the arcade, where flashing lights and cheerful music filled the air. Henry challenged Evan to a round of pinball, while William and Michael teamed up for a competitive game of racing simulators. Laughter echoed through the room as the children tried their hand at skee-ball and whack-a-mole.

Outside, the carousel twirled gracefully, its painted horses carrying delighted children on a journey of whimsy. Elizabeth and Charlie eagerly waited their turn, their giggles rising above the gentle hum of the diner.Amidst the excitement, William and Henry led their families to the creative workshop – a haven of imagination and artistic expression nestled in a cozy corner of Fredbear's. Here, children could unleash their creativity through various crafts and activities.

"Let's see what masterpieces we can create today!" Henry exclaimed, handing out aprons and paintbrushes to the eager children.

Under the guidance of their fathers, the children painted vibrant murals, crafted friendship bracelets, and molded clay sculptures of Fredbear and Spring Bonnie. Elizabeth and Charlie collaborated on a colorful banner that read 'Friendship Forever', while Evan proudly presented his clay figurine of Fredbear to William.

"This is for you, Dad," Evan beamed, his eyes shining with pride.

William ruffled Evan's hair affectionately. "Thank you, son. It's wonderful."

The workshop buzzed with creativity and camaraderie as the families bonded over their shared love for art and imagination.As the afternoon sun began its descent, William and Henry suggested a picnic under the shade of a majestic oak tree that graced the diner's garden. They spread out checkered blankets and unpacked a feast of sandwiches, fresh fruit, and homemade treats prepared by Mrs. Emily and Mrs. Afton.

"Remember our old picnics, Henry?" William mused, a nostalgic smile gracing his face as he glanced around at the familiar surroundings.

Henry nodded, his gaze drifting over the happy faces of their children. "Those were simpler times. But today, we're making new memories with our families."

The children, their laughter blending with the rustling leaves overhead, savored the delicious food and the company of their parents and friends. They recounted their favorite moments of the day – from arcade victories to artistic triumphs – and eagerly planned their next adventure at Fredbear's.As dusk painted the sky in hues of pink and gold, William and Henry ushered their families to the main stage for the grand finale of the day – a magical puppet show starring Fredbear and Spring Bonnie. The children gathered in awe as the animatronics came to life, their voices filled with warmth and charm as they told stories of courage, kindness, and the power of friendship.

William and Henry watched with pride as their children laughed and clapped, completely captivated by the enchanting performance. The puppet show, with its whimsical characters and heartfelt messages, reminded everyone of the joy and wonder that Fredbear's Family Diner brought to their lives.As the puppet show drew to a close, the Afton and Emily families bid farewell to Fredbear's Family Diner with hearts full of happiness and memories that would last a lifetime. They thanked their guests and employees for a day filled with laughter, fun, and the magic of childhood.

"Thank you for joining us today," William said warmly, shaking hands with the diner's staff. "It was a day to remember."

Henry nodded, his heart overflowing with gratitude. "Indeed, William. Let's make it a tradition to celebrate like this every year."

As they drove home, the families reflected on the day's events with smiles and contentment. They knew that Fredbear's Family Diner was more than just a place of business – it was a testament to their friendship, their dedication to creating joy, and the love they shared with their families.

THE EASTER EGG HUNT AT FREDBEAR'S FAMILY DINER

Spring had arrived in the quiet town where Fredbear's Family Diner stood, its colorful sign welcoming patrons with a cheerful greeting. Inside, the air was filled with the scent of freshly baked pies and the soft hum of laughter as families gathered for the annual Easter egg hunt.

Among the crowd was Cassidy, a young boy with bright blonde hair that caught the sunlight and eyes filled with wonder. He clutched a woven basket tightly in one hand, his excitement palpable as he waited for the festivities to begin.

Beside him stood Evan Afton, his best friend and constant companion. Evan, with his tousled brown hair and a smile that could light up the darkest of rooms, shared Cassidy's enthusiasm for the day's events. Together, they scanned the diner's interior, eager to spot their favorite animatronics, Spring Bonnie and Fredbear.

Spring Bonnie, a charming animatronic with soft pastel colors and a friendly demeanor, greeted children with a gentle wave and a reassuring smile. Fredbear, towering and golden with a jovial demeanor, chuckled warmly as he entertained guests with magic tricks and songs.

The diner buzzed with excitement as children and parents alike gathered for the Easter egg hunt. Cassidy and Evan joined the throng of eager participants, their eyes scanning the diner's nooks and crannies in search of hidden treasures.

"Think we'll find the golden egg this year?" Cassidy whispered eagerly to Evan, his voice tinged with excitement.

Evan shrugged, his gaze fixed on a cluster of potted plants near the entrance. "Who knows? Maybe we'll get lucky."

With a signal from the diner's manager, the Easter egg hunt commenced. Children scattered in every direction, their laughter echoing off the diner's walls as they searched high and low for brightly colored eggs hidden among the tables and chairs.

Cassidy and Evan darted through the diner, their laughter mingling with the joyous cries of their peers. They checked beneath tables, behind curtains, and even ventured near Spring Bonnie and Fredbear, who watched over the festivities with a fondness that only animatronics could muster.

In their quest for eggs, Cassidy stumbled upon a hidden alcove tucked away behind a curtain near the stage. He gasped in delight as he discovered a cluster of golden eggs nestled among plush toys and party favors. "Evan, look!" Cassidy called out excitedly, waving his friend over.

Evan hurried to Cassidy's side, his eyes widening in awe at the sight of the golden eggs. "Wow, we found them!"

The two friends carefully collected the golden eggs, placing them gently in Cassidy's basket as they shared excited whispers about their good fortune. Their laughter drew the attention of Spring Bonnie and Fredbear, who approached with a curious tilt of their robotic heads.

"Well done, young adventurers!" Fredbear boomed jovially, his voice carrying across the diner. "You've found the golden eggs. A reward awaits you!"

Spring Bonnie knelt beside Cassidy and Evan, his soft fur shimmering in the soft glow of the diner's lights. "You've made quite the discovery," he chimed in with a warm smile. "Perhaps you'll uncover even more surprises as the day unfolds."

As Cassidy and Evan reveled in their victory, William Afton, the diner's owner and a kind-hearted man with a gentle demeanor, approached the group with a tray of freshly baked cookies. "Congratulations, boys! Looks like you've had quite the adventure," he remarked warmly, his gaze filled with pride for the two friends.

Cassidy beamed up at William, sharing the tale of their discovery with enthusiasm. William listened attentively, his laughter blending with the cheerful chatter of the diner as families gathered around to celebrate the day's successes.

As the Easter egg hunt drew to a close, families bid farewell to Spring Bonnie and Fredbear, their hearts lighter and spirits lifted by the magic of the day. Cassidy and Evan exchanged a final wave with their favorite animatronics, already looking forward to the next adventure they would share together.

And so, as the stars twinkled overhead and the diner slowly emptied, Cassidy and Evan cherished the memory of their Easter egg hunt at Fredbear's Family Diner—a day filled with friendship, discovery, and the timeless magic of Spring Bonnie, Fredbear, and a kind-hearted owner's encouragement.

In this version William Afton is portrayed as the owner of Fredbear's Family Diner, adding warmth and encouragement to Cassidy and Evan's adventure at the diner.

A DAY IN THE AFTON HOUSEHOLD

In a quiet suburban neighborhood, nestled amidst tall trees and blooming gardens, stood the Afton household – a cozy, two-story home that exuded warmth and comfort. Inside, the Afton family lived their lives with a sense of normalcy that belied the mysteries and dark tales often associated with their name.The sun peeked through the curtains of Michael Afton's bedroom, gently rousing him from his slumber. Stretching lazily, he yawned and glanced at the clock – it was early, but he could already hear the faint sounds of his younger brother Evan's laughter echoing from downstairs.

Downstairs in the kitchen, Mrs. Clara Afton, a kind-hearted woman with a passion for baking, was already busy preparing breakfast. The aroma of freshly brewed coffee and sizzling bacon filled the air, mingling with the scent of homemade blueberry muffins – Evan's favorite.

"Good morning, sleepyhead," Clara greeted Michael with a warm smile as he entered the kitchen. "Care for some pancakes?"

Michael grinned, taking a seat at the table. "You know it, Mom."

As they ate breakfast together, Michael shared stories of his upcoming school projects and weekend plans with his friends. Clara listened attentively, offering words of encouragement and occasionally stealing a glance at her husband, William Afton, who sat quietly reading the morning newspaper.William Afton, a man of few words but deep convictions, owned a small workshop in the backyard where he spent hours tinkering with animatronics and other mechanical devices. To Michael, his father was a source of both awe and inspiration – a brilliant inventor whose creations had earned him recognition in the local community.

"Dad, can I help you with the animatronics today?" Michael asked eagerly, finishing his breakfast.

William looked up from his workbench, his eyes crinkling in a smile. "Sure thing, champ. Grab your toolbox."

Together, father and son spent the morning fine-tuning Freddy Fazbear, an animatronic bear that William had designed for a local children's entertainment venue. Michael marveled at his father's ingenuity, asking questions and learning the intricacies of mechanical engineering.

"You're a natural, Michael," William praised, patting his son on the back. "One day, this workshop will be yours."Meanwhile, Evan Afton, the youngest member of the family, was busy exploring the backyard with their loyal golden retriever, Freddy. Evan had inherited his father's curiosity and knack for tinkering, often building makeshift forts and imaginary worlds out of cardboard boxes and old toys.

"Look, Freddy! I made us a spaceship!" Evan exclaimed proudly, climbing into a large box adorned with colorful markers.

Freddy barked in agreement, wagging his tail as he joined Evan in their space exploration mission. The backyard echoed with their laughter and playful banter, a testament to the bond between a boy and his faithful companion.

Inside, Elizabeth Afton, the eldest sibling, sat at her desk in her bedroom, surrounded by sketchbooks and art supplies. An aspiring artist with a talent for capturing emotions in her drawings, Elizabeth found solace in her creative pursuits and often sought inspiration from the world around her – including the animatronics her father crafted with such care.After a morning filled with laughter and creativity, the Afton family gathered for a leisurely lunch in the backyard garden. They spread a checkered blanket on the grass and enjoyed a picnic-style feast of sandwiches, fresh fruit, and Clara's famous lemonade.

"Dad, Mom, guess what?" Michael announced excitedly between bites of his sandwich. "I got an A on my science project!"

Clara clapped her hands in delight. "That's wonderful, Michael! I knew you could do it."

William nodded approvingly. "Keep up the good work, son. Science is the key to unlocking new possibilities."

As they chatted and savored their meal, the Afton family basked in the simple joys of togetherness – sharing stories, making plans for the weekend, and enjoying the sunshine that bathed their garden in a golden glow.As the afternoon turned to evening, the Afton family gathered in the living room for their evening traditions. They curled up on the couch, popcorn in hand, and watched classic movies that had become a beloved part of their family routine.

"Tonight's movie is 'The Adventures of Freddy and Friends,'" William announced, inserting the DVD into the player.

Evan clapped his hands eagerly. "I love Freddy and Friends!"

The movie filled the room with laughter and excitement as the animated characters – inspired by the animatronics at William's workshop – embarked on thrilling adventures and learned valuable lessons about friendship and bravery.As bedtime approached, Clara tucked Evan into bed and read him a bedtime story from his favorite book. The story, filled with whimsical creatures and magical lands, transported Evan to a world of dreams and possibilities.

"Goodnight, Mom," Evan murmured sleepily, hugging his stuffed Freddy bear close.

Clara kissed his forehead gently. "Sweet dreams, my little explorer."

Upstairs, Michael and Elizabeth shared stories of their day before settling into their own beds. William joined Clara in their bedroom, where they talked about their hopes and dreams for their children – a future filled with happiness, success, and boundless opportunities.As the night settled over the Afton household, a sense of peace and contentment filled the air. In their own unique ways, each member of the family contributed to the legacy of love, creativity, and resilience that defined the Afton name.

Outside, under the watchful gaze of the stars, Freddy Fazbear stood silent in William's workshop, a testament to the family's shared passion for bringing joy to others through their creations.

As they drifted off to sleep, the Afton family knew that no matter what challenges the future held, they would face them together – united by their love for each other and the unwavering belief that with love and determination, anything was possible.

UNEXPECTED FRIENDSHIP

It was another bustling monday afternoon at Freddy Fazbear's Pizza, where the air was filled with the sound of laughter and the enticing aroma of pizza. Cassidy, with a bright smile , was particularly excited. He had been looking forward to this day all week – a day to immerse himself in the fun and magic of the pizzeria.

Cassidy loved everything about Freddy Fazbear's Pizza: the games, the animatronics, and, most importantly, the delicious pizza. Today, he had his sights set on winning as many tickets as possible to trade for a special prize he had been eyeing – a limited-edition Freddy Fazbear plushie.

As he darted from game to game, his pockets gradually filled with tickets. He was determined to get that plushie, no matter how many skee-ball games he had to play. Cassidy was just about to start another game when he noticed someone he hadn't seen before: a man with thinning hair and a kind, if slightly weary, smile. He wore a purple uniform with a name tag that read "William."

William Afton had been working at Freddy Fazbear's Pizza for a few months now. He was responsible for maintaining the animatronics and ensuring everything ran smoothly. Despite the challenges of his job, he found joy in seeing the children's faces light up with happiness.

Cassidy, being the curious boy he was, approached William. "Hi! I'm Cassidy. Are you new here? I haven't seen you around before."

William smiled warmly at the boy. "Hello, Cassidy. I'm William. I've been working here for a little while, mostly behind the scenes. How are you enjoying your day?"

"It's great! I'm trying to win enough tickets for that Freddy plushie over there," Cassidy said, pointing towards the prize counter.

William glanced at the plushie and then back at Cassidy. "That's a fine prize. You know, I might have a few tips to help you win more tickets. Would you like some help?"

Cassidy's eyes lit up with excitement. "Really? That would be awesome!" William guided Cassidy to a nearby game, the classic whack-a-mole. "Alright, Cassidy, the key to this game is to stay focused and use both hands. Don't just whack randomly; try to anticipate where the moles will pop up next."

Cassidy followed William's advice, concentrating hard. To his delight, he started racking up tickets faster than ever. William moved with him from game to game, offering advice and encouragement. Cassidy felt like he had his own personal coach, and his ticket collection grew rapidly.

Between games, they chatted about the animatronics and the pizzeria. Cassidy was fascinated by William's stories about how the animatronics worked and how much care went into keeping them in tip-top shape.

"You know, Cassidy, the animatronics have a lot of moving parts and need constant attention. But seeing kids like you having fun makes it all worthwhile," William said, smiling at the boy's enthusiasm. As the day went on, Cassidy realized he had more than enough tickets for the plushie. He eagerly handed them to the prize counter attendant and clutched his new Freddy plushie tightly. "Thank you, Mr. William! I couldn't have done it without you."

William chuckled. "It was my pleasure, Cassidy. I'm glad I could help."

Cassidy's eyes sparkled with gratitude. "Hey, do you think we could take a picture together with Freddy? You know, to remember this day?"

William hesitated for a moment but then nodded. "Sure, Cassidy. Let's do it."

They found a spot near the stage where Freddy and the gang performed. Cassidy held up his plushie, and with a little help from one of the staff, they snapped a photo. Cassidy beamed with joy, and even William looked genuinely happy.

As the day drew to a close, William had one more surprise for Cassidy. "There's something special I'd like to show you, Cassidy. Follow me."

Intrigued, Cassidy followed William to a small room behind the stage. Inside was a miniature version of Freddy Fazbear's Pizza, complete with tiny animatronics and a working stage. "Wow! This is amazing!" Cassidy exclaimed, eyes wide with wonder.

William smiled. "I built this a while ago. It's a little project of mine. I thought you might like to see it."

Cassidy carefully examined the miniature setup, admiring the detail and craftsmanship. "You're really talented, Mr. William. Thank you for showing me this."

William placed a hand on Cassidy's shoulder. "I'm glad you enjoyed it. It's always nice to share something special with someone who appreciates it."As the pizzeria began to close for the night, Cassidy knew it was time to go. He hugged his Freddy plushie tightly and looked up at William. "Today was the best day ever. Thank you for everything, Mr. William."

William smiled warmly. "I'm glad you had a good time, Cassidy. Remember, you're always welcome here at Freddy Fazbear's Pizza."

Cassidy waved goodbye and made his way to the exit, where his parents were waiting. "Mom! Dad! I had the most amazing day! And look, I got the Freddy plushie!"

As Cassidy and his family left, William watched them go with a contented smile. Helping Cassidy had reminded him why he loved working at Freddy Fazbear's Pizza. It was a place where joy and fun were the order of the day, and where unexpected friendships could blossom.The next day, as Cassidy eagerly showed his friends the photo and recounted his adventure, he couldn't wait to return `to Freddy Fazbear's Pizza. He knew that there would be more fun, more games, and hopefully, more time spent with his new friend, William.

William, meanwhile, went back to his duties with a lighter heart. He looked forward to the next time he'd see Cassidy and the other children whose laughter filled the pizzeria with life.

In a place where the magic of childhood and the joy of playfulness thrived, Cassidy and William had found a special connection. And as long as there were children to delight and stories to be shared, Freddy Fazbear's Pizza would always be a place of wonder and happiness.

THE ADVENTURES OF CASSIDY AND EVAN

Cassidy and Evan Afton were inseparable friends, their bond forged through shared adventures and a love for exploring the mysteries that surrounded their small town. Cassidy, with his bright blonde hair that seemed to catch the sunlight and a mischievous sparkle in his eyes, was always the instigator of their escapades.

One crisp autumn afternoon, Cassidy burst through the old iron gates of the Afton estate, his laughter echoing through the quiet grounds. Evan, a quieter boy with tousled brown hair and a curious nature, followed close behind, a small leather-bound notebook tucked under his arm.

"C'mon, Evan! I heard there's a secret passage in the garden," Cassidy exclaimed, his excitement palpable.

Evan raised an eyebrow skeptically. "Are you sure? My dad says the estate has been here for centuries. I don't think there's anything we haven't explored already."

Cassidy grinned mischievously. "That's what makes it exciting! Imagine finding something no one else has seen in years."

With a shared sense of adventure, the boys set off through the meticulously trimmed hedges and sprawling rose bushes that lined the estate's garden. The air was crisp with the scent of fallen leaves and the promise of discovery.

As they ventured deeper into the garden, Cassidy's keen eyes spotted a peculiar arrangement of stones near the base of a towering oak tree. "Look, Evan! I think this might be it," Cassidy whispered excitedly, his voice barely above a breath.

Evan approached cautiously, his curiosity piqued. Together, they pushed aside the overgrown ivy and revealed a hidden trapdoor nestled beneath the tree's gnarled roots. With a glance filled with excitement and anticipation, Cassidy turned to Evan, his eyes sparkling with mischief.

"Shall we?" Cassidy asked, a daring grin spreading across his face.

Evan hesitated for a moment, then nodded eagerly. With Cassidy leading the way, they descended into the darkness below, their footsteps echoing against stone walls lined with flickering torches.

The tunnel twisted and turned, leading them deeper into the heart of the Afton estate than they had ever ventured before. They discovered forgotten chambers filled with dusty relics of a bygone era—old paintings that seemed to watch their every move and ancient suits of armor that stood silent sentinels in the dim light.

Hours passed in a blur as Cassidy and Evan explored the labyrinthine passages, their excitement mounting with each new discovery. They uncovered hidden libraries filled with crumbling books and whispered legends of ghosts that haunted the halls of the mansion.

As dusk settled over the estate, casting long shadows across the garden, Cassidy and Evan emerged from the secret tunnel, their hearts racing with the thrill of their adventure. They exchanged a silent glance, their friendship strengthened by the shared moments of excitement and danger.

"We should keep this our secret," Evan suggested softly, his voice filled with a mix of awe and reverence for the mysteries they had uncovered.

Cassidy nodded in agreement, a grin spreading across his face. "Definitely. But you know, there's still so much more to explore."

And with that promise hanging in the air, Cassidy and Evan Afton retreated back into the comforting embrace of the Afton estate, their friendship bound by the unspoken vow to continue their adventures together, wherever their curiosity led them next.

In the quiet corners of the Afton estate, amidst secrets and shadows, Cassidy and Evan's friendship thrived, their shared explorations becoming the stuff of whispered tales and cherished memories for years to come.

A DAY OF FUN AT CIRCUS BABY'S PIZZA WORLD

It was a bright and sunny Saturday, and the doors of Circus Baby's Pizza World swung open with a cheerful chime. Inside, the air was filled with the aroma of freshly baked pizza and the excited chatter of children. Today was special—it was Suzie's birthday, and her parents had planned a surprise party at her favorite place in town.

Suzie, a spirited eight-year-old with a love for adventure and a heart full of curiosity, arrived at Circus Baby's Pizza World with her friends, Abby and Cassidy. Their eyes sparkled with anticipation as they entered the colorful dining area adorned with balloons, streamers, and posters featuring Circus Baby, Ballora, and Funtime Freddy.

Circus Baby herself greeted the children with a warm smile from the stage. "Welcome, Suzie!" she said in her gentle voice over the speakers. "Are you ready for a day filled with fun and surprises?"

Suzie's face lit up with excitement as she nodded enthusiastically. Circus Baby waved a mechanical hand, inviting Suzie and her friends to explore the arcade games and attractions. Abby and Cassidy dashed towards the carousel and bumper cars, eager to start their adventure, while Suzie lingered near the stage, watching Ballora and Funtime Freddy perform their graceful dances.

Ballora, with her elegant movements and twinkling eyes, noticed Suzie watching and glided over gracefully. "Hello, birthday girl! Would you like to join us for a dance?" Suzie giggled and nodded, swaying to the enchanting music as she joined Ballora and Funtime Freddy in a mesmerizing dance. The other children in the pizzeria clapped and cheered, captivated by the elegant performance.

After the dance, Suzie rejoined Abby and Cassidy, and together they explored the various arcade games. They raced in the virtual reality simulators, tested their aim at the shooting gallery, and challenged each other to games of skill and agility. With each game won, they earned more tokens, adding to the growing pile for the prize counter.

Meanwhile, in the kitchen, Funtime Foxy the energetic fox animatronic and their assistant, Bon-Bon, were busy preparing Suzie's favorite pizza—a delicious blend of cheese, bacon, and extra olives. The kitchen buzzed with excitement as Funtime Foxy sang cheerfully while Bon-Bon cracked jokes and kept the kitchen staff entertained.

As Suzie and her friends enjoyed their gaming spree, they were surprised by Circus Baby herself, who appeared with a tray of delightful cupcakes decorated with sprinkles in Circus Baby's signature colors. "Happy birthday, Suzie!" Circus Baby exclaimed warmly, her eyes sparkling with joy as she handed Suzie the tray. Suzie's heart swelled with happiness as she thanked Circus Baby and shared the cupcakes with Abby and Cassidy.

After the cupcakes, it was time for the highlight of the day—the animatronic show on the main stage. Suzie and her friends found front-row seats as Circus Baby, Ballora, and Funtime Freddy took the stage, performing Suzie's favorite songs and dazzling dance routines. The children clapped and sang along, enchanted by the colorful lights and lively music.

As the show concluded, Circus Baby invited Suzie on stage for a special birthday surprise. With a flourish of confetti and cheers from the audience, Circus Baby presented Suzie with a giant plush Circus Baby doll and a stack of tokens for the prize counter. Suzie beamed with delight, hugging her new plush friend tightly as she thanked Circus Baby, Ballora, and Funtime Freddy for the unforgettable day.

With the afternoon drawing to a close, Suzie and her friends collected their prizes from the counter—a mix of plush toys, action figures, and colorful novelties—and bid farewell to their animatronic friends. As they exited Circus Baby's Pizza World, Suzie turned to her parents with a wide grin. "This was the best birthday ever!" she exclaimed, her heart filled with happiness and memories to cherish.

As they drove home, Suzie held her plush Circus Baby doll close, already planning her next visit to Circus Baby's Pizza World. For Suzie, and for every child who entered through those doors, Circus Baby's Pizza World was more than just a pizzeria—it was a place where dreams came true, laughter echoed through the halls, and friendships blossomed in the enchanting world of animatronic wonders.

EVAN'S REDEMPTION: A TALE OF FORGIVENESS

It had been years since the tragic incidents at Freddy Fazbear's Pizza, but the memories still haunted Evan Afton. Night after night, he was tormented by visions of the animatronics – twisted, nightmarish versions that seemed to embody his deepest fears. These were not the friendly characters he had once known but monstrous beings that haunted his dreams.

Evan knew that the only way to find peace was to confront these nightmares head-on. One evening, he made a decision. He would return to the place where it all began – the now-abandoned Fazbear's Fright. It was here that he hoped to find closure and, perhaps, a way to reconcile with the nightmares that plagued him.Evan arrived at Fazbear's Fright as the sun set, casting long shadows over the dilapidated building. The air was thick with the scent of decay and old memories. Taking a deep breath, he pushed open the creaky door and stepped inside.

The interior was dark, lit only by the faint glow of his flashlight. Evan's footsteps echoed as he made his way through the corridors, each step bringing back a flood of memories – both good and bad. He passed by old arcade machines, torn posters, and empty stages, each a ghost of the past.

As he ventured deeper into the building, he felt an eerie presence. The air grew colder, and the shadows seemed to move on their own. Evan's heart pounded in his chest, but he pressed on, determined to face whatever lay ahead.Evan reached the main attraction: the maze of horror-themed rooms where the Nightmare Animatronics awaited. He could feel their presence, watching him from the darkness. Taking a deep breath, he called out, "I'm not here to fight. I'm here to make peace."

For a moment, there was silence. Then, the darkness seemed to ripple, and the Nightmares emerged. First came Nightmare Freddy, his eyes glowing menacingly. Then Nightmare Bonnie, Nightmare Chica, and finally, the most terrifying of all, Nightmare Fredbear.

Evan stood his ground, trying to keep his fear in check. "I know I've made mistakes," he began, his voice trembling slightly. "I know I hurt you, and I'm sorry. I was just a kid, and I didn't understand what was happening. But I want to make things right."

Nightmare Fredbear stepped forward, his towering figure casting a shadow over Evan. "Why should we believe you?" he growled, his voice deep and foreboding.

Evan took a deep breath. "Because I'm not the same person I was back then. I've changed. I want to help you find peace, just like I want to find peace for myself." To Evan's surprise, the Nightmares didn't attack. Instead, they seemed to consider his words. Nightmare Bonnie, his ears twitching, spoke next. "How can you help us? We're trapped in this endless cycle of torment."

Evan thought for a moment. "Maybe we can start by understanding each other. You're part of my nightmares, but you were once part of something good too. Maybe if we remember those good times, we can find a way to move forward."

Nightmare Chica, her beak glinting in the dim light, tilted her head. "You mean… like the pizza parties and the laughter?"

Evan nodded. "Exactly. We can't change the past, but we can choose to remember the good times and let go of the pain." The Nightmares seemed to soften at Evan's words. Together, they began to recall the happier moments from their past. Nightmare Freddy remembered the joy of performing on stage, hearing the children's laughter. Nightmare Bonnie recalled playing music that made everyone smile. Nightmare Chica reminisced about the endless pizza parties and the fun they had.

Even Nightmare Fredbear, the most fearsome of them all, remembered a time when he brought joy instead of fear. "We were happy once," he said quietly. "Maybe we can be happy again."

Evan felt a warmth spread through him. "We can. It won't be easy, but if we work together, we can find a way to heal."Over the next few weeks, Evan returned to Fazbear's Fright regularly. Each time, he spent more time with the Nightmares, helping them to reclaim their happier memories. They cleaned up the old building, restoring it to its former glory. They even set up a small stage and performed together, just like they used to.

The more they worked together, the more the Nightmares began to change. Their terrifying appearances softened, and they started to resemble their original, friendly selves. The bonds they formed with Evan grew stronger, built on mutual understanding and forgiveness.

One evening, as they finished another performance, Nightmare Fredbear – now simply Fredbear – turned to Evan. "Thank you," he said sincerely. "You've given us a chance to be happy again."

Evan smiled, tears glistening in his eyes. "And you've given me the peace I've been searching for. Thank you for forgiving me."Fazbear's Fright was no longer a place of fear and torment. It had become a place of joy and reconciliation, where Evan and the animatronics could create new, happy memories together. The nightmares that once haunted Evan were gone, replaced by a sense of peace and fulfillment.

Evan knew that the road to healing was long, but with his new friends by his side, he felt ready to face whatever the future held. As he stood on the stage, looking out at the animatronics – his friends – he felt a warmth in his heart.

"Here's to new beginnings," he said, raising a cup of soda. The animatronics raised their cups in return, their eyes shining with hope and happiness.

And so, in a place that had once been filled with darkness and fear, there was now light and joy. Evan and the animatronics had found forgiveness and friendship, proving that even the deepest wounds could heal with time, understanding, and a little bit of heart.

SPRINGTRAP'S UNEXPECTED DAY OF FUN AT FAZBEAR'S FRIGHT

In the dark, dusty corridors of Fazbear's Fright: The Horror Attraction, an eerie silence reigned. Once a place of fear and mystery, it was now abandoned, its animatronics dormant and its hallways echoing with the whispers of the past. Among the relics of this haunted attraction lay Springtrap, an animatronic suit with a dark history. Yet, today was a day unlike any other.

As the first light of dawn crept through the broken windows, a flicker of life stirred within Springtrap. For reasons unknown, the ancient mechanisms within the animatronic sparked to life. His eyes glowed dimly, and with a slow, creaky motion, Springtrap rose from his long slumber.

"Where am I?" Springtrap muttered to himself, looking around the derelict attraction. His memory was hazy, but one thing was clear: this place was no longer filled with screams of terror, but with a strange, inviting warmth.Curiosity got the better of him, and Springtrap began to explore the attraction. He wandered through the darkened halls, passing by old posters of Freddy Fazbear and his friends, tattered banners, and empty arcade machines. As he moved, a peculiar sound reached his ears – the distant hum of carnival music and the joyful laughter of children.

Guided by these sounds, Springtrap made his way to the main attraction area. To his surprise, the scene before him was nothing like the abandoned halls he had traversed. The area was bustling with activity, filled with children playing games, families enjoying snacks, and animatronics entertaining the crowd.

At the center of it all was a stage, where Freddy, Bonnie, Chica, and Foxy were performing a lively show. The audience clapped and sang along, their faces alight with joy.

Springtrap watched from the shadows, feeling a mixture of awe and confusion. "This place... it's so different," he whispered. His curiosity piqued, he decided to step out of the darkness and into the light.As Springtrap approached the crowd, the children's laughter turned into gasps of surprise. They stared at the tattered, greenish animatronic, unsure what to make of him. Sensing their apprehension, Freddy paused the performance and approached Springtrap with a friendly smile.

"Hey there, friend! Welcome to the show!" Freddy said, extending a hand.

Springtrap hesitated, then shook Freddy's hand. "I'm... Springtrap. I didn't mean to scare anyone. I just woke up and heard the music."

Freddy's smile widened. "No worries, Springtrap. We're all about fun and games here! Why don't you join us? There's plenty of fun to be had."

The children, seeing Freddy's acceptance of Springtrap, quickly warmed up to the newcomer. They crowded around him, eager to show him their favorite games and activities.Springtrap found himself being led by a group of excited children to various attractions. First, they took him to the arcade, where they showed him how to play games like Skee-Ball and Whack-a-Mole. Though his movements were stiff and awkward at first, Springtrap quickly got the hang of it, much to the delight of the kids.

"Look, Springtrap! You got the high score!" one of the children cheered as Springtrap successfully beat the top score on a racing game.

Next, they headed to the prize booth, where Springtrap used the tickets he had won to get a small plushie of himself. The sight of the plushie made him chuckle, and he carefully tucked it under his arm.

The group then moved to the dining area, where Chica served them pizza. Springtrap watched in amazement as the children devoured the slices with gusto. Chica handed him a slice, and though he couldn't eat it himself, he appreciated the gesture.As the day went on, Springtrap felt a sense of joy he had never known. The children's laughter and the friendly atmosphere made him feel welcome and accepted. Freddy, noticing how much the kids enjoyed Springtrap's company, had an idea.

"Hey, Springtrap, how about you join our performance? I think the kids would love to see you on stage with us," Freddy suggested.

Springtrap was hesitant. "I've never performed before. I'm not sure if I can do it."

Freddy placed a reassuring hand on his shoulder. "Don't worry. We'll be right there with you. Just follow our lead and have fun!"

Taking a deep breath, Springtrap agreed. As the sun began to set, the animatronics prepared for the evening show. The stage was set, the lights dimmed, and the music started. Freddy, Bonnie, Chica, and Foxy took their places, and Springtrap joined them, feeling a mix of excitement and nervousness.The curtain rose, and the crowd cheered as the animatronics began their performance. Springtrap followed Freddy's lead, moving in time with the music. To his surprise, he found that he enjoyed dancing and singing along.

The children in the audience clapped and cheered, thrilled to see Springtrap on stage. As the performance continued, Springtrap's confidence grew. He even added his own flair to the routine, eliciting laughter and applause from the crowd.

At the end of the show, the animatronics took their bows, and Springtrap received a standing ovation. He looked out at the sea of smiling faces and felt a warmth in his heart.After the show, Springtrap and the other animatronics gathered backstage. Freddy patted him on the back. "You did great, Springtrap! The kids loved you."

Springtrap smiled, feeling a sense of belonging he had never experienced before. "Thank you, Freddy. I never thought I could have so much fun."

Bonnie and Chica joined in, congratulating Springtrap on his performance. Foxy, with a mischievous grin, handed him a pirate hat. "Arr, welcome to the crew, matey!" he said, winking.

As the night came to an end, Springtrap reflected on the day's events. He had gone from a forgotten relic to a beloved member of the Fazbear family. The darkness that had once consumed him was replaced by light, laughter, and friendship.In the days that followed, Springtrap became a regular part of the entertainment at Fazbear's Fright. He learned new routines, played more games, and continued to bond with the children and his fellow animatronics.

The once-abandoned attraction was now a place of joy and fun, where Springtrap found a new purpose. He was no longer defined by his past but by the happiness he brought to others.

One evening, as the animatronics prepared for another performance, Springtrap looked around at his friends and the excited children in the audience. He felt a sense of fulfillment and gratitude.

"Ready for another great show, Springtrap?" Freddy asked, smiling.

Springtrap nodded, his eyes shining with joy. "Absolutely. Let's make some more happy memories."

The curtain rose, and the show began. The music played, the animatronics danced, and the crowd cheered. Springtrap felt a warmth in his heart, knowing that he had found a new family and a place where he truly belonged.

As the stars twinkled in the night sky, Springtrap realized that he had been given a second chance. A chance to bring joy instead of fear, to create happy memories instead of nightmares.

And so, with a heart full of happiness and a spirit renewed, Springtrap embraced his new life at Fazbear's Fright, where every day was a new adventure, and every smile was a testament to the power of forgiveness and fun.

A GATHERING OF FAMILIES

The sun beamed down on the sprawling gardens of both the Afton and Emily estates, where vibrant flowers bloomed and towering trees provided shade. Today was a special day, marked by the anticipation of a grand garden party that had been meticulously planned by both families – a celebration of friendship, love, and the joy of being together.At the Afton estate, Mrs. Afton and her children – Michael, Elizabeth, and Evan – were busy with last-minute preparations. Mrs. Afton, with her love for gardening, had spent days ensuring the garden was in perfect condition. Colorful banners fluttered in the gentle breeze, and tables adorned with floral centerpieces were set up under the shade of large umbrellas.

William Afton, their father, was helping out with setting up the barbecue and ensuring everything was in place for the guests. Michael, the eldest Afton sibling, was organizing games and activities, while Elizabeth and Evan were putting the finishing touches on handmade decorations.

"Mom, Dad, do you think everything looks alright?" Elizabeth asked, tying a ribbon onto a banner that read 'Welcome Friends'.

Mrs. Afton smiled warmly. "It looks wonderful, dear. Your father and I are very proud of all your hard work. I'm sure our guests will love it."

Evan, the youngest Afton sibling, nodded enthusiastically. "I can't wait to see everyone again! Do you think Henry will like the surprise we have for him?"

William Afton chuckled softly. "I'm sure he will, Evan. The Emily family is looking forward to this just as much as we are."

As they made final adjustments, the Afton family eagerly awaited the arrival of their friends.Meanwhile, at the Emily estate, Mr. and Mrs. Emily were busy with their own preparations for the garden party. Henry Emily, an excellent cook and gardener, was tending to the barbecue and preparing delicious dishes using fresh produce from their garden. The smell of grilled meats and vegetables filled the air, promising a delightful feast for their guests.

Mrs. Emily, known for her artistic talents, was setting up a display of handmade crafts and floral arrangements. Their children – Sammy and Charlie – were helping by arranging seating areas and setting up games like croquet and horseshoes on the well-manicured lawn.

"Dad, do you think the Aftons will like the surprise cookies we made?" Charlie asked, placing a tray of freshly baked treats on the buffet table.

"I'm sure they'll love them," Mr. Emily replied with a grin, ruffling Charlie's hair affectionately. "It's going to be a fantastic day. Let's make sure everything is perfect."

As the Emily family made final preparations, they couldn't contain their excitement for the celebration ahead. As the clock struck noon, the first guests began to arrive at the Afton estate. The Emily family followed shortly after, greeted warmly by the Aftons at the garden gate. William Afton and Henry Emily exchanged hearty handshakes and shared laughs, happy to reunite with old friends.

"Welcome, welcome!" Mrs. Afton exclaimed, leading them into the garden where tables were laden with refreshments and colorful decorations adorned every corner.

The children wasted no time in running off to explore the garden together, their laughter echoing through the air. Sammy and Michael quickly bonded over their mutual love for video games, while Charlie and Elizabeth chatted animatedly about their favorite books. The garden party was in full swing as guests mingled, enjoying delicious food and participating in various activities. Mr. Emily took charge of the barbecue, grilling meats to perfection while Mrs. Afton and Mrs. Emily caught up over cups of tea, sharing stories and laughter.

Meanwhile, the children played games and enjoyed the sunny afternoon. They swung on the swings, played tag among the trees, and even organized a friendly game of soccer. Evan and Charlie teamed up for a scavenger hunt, while Elizabeth and Sammy explored a hidden pathway that led to a small pond.

As the day progressed, the garden echoed with joy and excitement, a testament to the bonds of friendship and the happiness shared between the two families.As the afternoon sun began to dip towards the horizon, the Afton and Emily families gathered under a large oak tree at the heart of the garden. They shared stories and fond memories, reminiscing about the adventures they had shared over the years.

"Remember the time we went camping by the lake?" William Afton chuckled, glancing at Henry Emily. "Evan and Sammy couldn't stop chasing fireflies."

"And how about the time we all went on that road trip to the beach?" Mrs. Emily added, smiling warmly. "Elizabeth and Charlie made friends with everyone they met."

The children listened with wide-eyed wonder, captivated by tales of their parents' youthful escapades. They felt a sense of belonging, knowing that their families' bond was built on a foundation of love, laughter, and shared experiences.As twilight painted the sky in hues of pink and orange, Mr. Emily suggested a surprise for their guests – a special performance by the children. Sammy, Charlie, Michael, Elizabeth, and Evan eagerly agreed, their excitement palpable.

Under the soft glow of string lights strung between the trees, the children gathered on a small stage they had set up earlier. They performed a medley of songs and dances they had rehearsed together, showcasing their talents and enthusiasm. Their parents watched with pride, clapping and cheering after each performance.

To everyone's delight, William Afton surprised them all by joining in with his guitar, adding a magical touch to the evening with his music. His melodies filled the garden with joyous tunes that spoke of love, friendship, and the beauty of togetherness.As the performances drew to a close, the Afton and Emily families gathered once more under the oak tree. They raised their glasses in a toast to friendship, family, and the bonds that united them.

"To the Aftons and the Emilys – may our friendship continue to grow and blossom," Henry Emily said, his voice filled with warmth.

"To the memories we've made and the ones yet to come," Mrs. Afton added, clinking her glass with Mrs. Emily's.

The children joined in the toast, their voices echoing the sentiments of their parents. They felt a deep sense of gratitude for the day they had shared, knowing that it was a day they would cherish forever.As the garden party came to an end, the Afton and Emily families bid each other farewell with hugs and promises to meet again soon. The children exchanged contact information, excited to stay in touch and plan future adventures together.

As they watched their guests depart, the Afton and Emily parents reflected on the day's events. They felt a renewed sense of gratitude for their friendships and a deep appreciation for the love that filled their lives.

"Today was truly magical," Mrs. Emily said, smiling at her family. "We should do this more often."

William Afton nodded in agreement. "Absolutely. Let's make it a tradition. There's nothing more precious than moments like these – surrounded by loved ones, sharing laughter and creating memories."

And so, under the stars and the gentle breeze of a summer evening, the Afton and Emily families said goodbye to a day filled with joy and looked forward to the promise of tomorrow, where new adventures and cherished memories awaited them.

A TEENAGER'S TALE

Life as a teenager in Hurricane, Utah is exactly what you'd expect - a mix of school, friends, and figuring out who I am in this world. My name is Michael Afton, and if there's one thing I've learned, it's that life is full of surprises, even in a small town like ours.Every day starts with the relentless buzzing of my alarm clock, followed by the struggle to drag myself out of bed. The sun streams through my window, painting the room in hues of gold and promising a new day filled with possibilities.

Downstairs, Mom's already in the kitchen, humming along to some old tune on the radio as she prepares breakfast. The smell of pancakes and freshly brewed coffee greets me as I stumble into the kitchen, still half-asleep.

"Morning, Michael," Mom greets me with a warm smile, placing a plate of pancakes in front of me. "Eat up. You've got a big day ahead."

I nod groggily, savoring the familiar taste of Mom's pancakes. After a quick breakfast and a gulp of orange juice, I grab my backpack and head out the door, ready to tackle whatever challenges await me at Hurricane High.Hurricane High School is a hive of activity as students hustle to their classes, gossip in the hallways, and prepare for the day ahead. For me, school is more than just academics - it's a place to catch up with friends, explore new interests, and maybe even figure out what I want to do with my life.

In between classes, I meet up with my best friend, Kyle. We've been inseparable since elementary school, bonding over video games, music, and our shared love for exploring abandoned places around town.

"Hey man, did you finish that history assignment?" Kyle asks, tossing me a grin as we walk to our next class.

I laugh, shaking my head. "Nah, I'm gonna wing it like always. How about you?"

Kyle shrugs. "Same here. Mrs. Johnson's not gonna know what hit her."

Together, we navigate the ups and downs of high school life, from surviving pop quizzes to cheering on our school's football team at Friday night games. Through it all, Kyle's always there with a joke or a reassuring pat on the back.After the final bell rings, signaling the end of another school day, I head to Freddy's Pizza Palace - a local hangout where the jukebox plays oldies, the pizza's always hot, and the arcade games never disappoint.

Freddy's is where I meet up with my circle of friends - Sarah, the aspiring artist with a penchant for drawing caricatures of our teachers; Alex, the math whiz who never misses a beat; and Emily, the bookworm who always has a new recommendation.

"Michael, you're late again," Sarah teases, handing me a slice of pepperoni pizza as I slide into the booth.

I grin sheepishly, taking a bite of the cheesy goodness. "Sorry, traffic was brutal."

We spend hours at Freddy's, sharing stories, debating the latest movies, and challenging each other to arcade tournaments. It's our sanctuary, where we can be ourselves without the pressures of school or family hovering over us.At home, family dinners are a lively affair. Dad, with his dry wit and endless supply of dad jokes, keeps us entertained while Mom fills our plates with her famous lasagna or tacos - comfort food that never fails to hit the spot.

"Michael, how was school today?" Dad asks, raising an eyebrow as he passes me the salad.

I shrug nonchalantly, pretending to ponder. "Eh, same old. You know how it is."

Mom chuckles, pouring herself a glass of wine. "You should talk to your sister more, Michael. She's dying to know what's going on in your life."

Elizabeth, my younger sister, shoots me a mischievous grin from across the table. At thirteen, she's already mastered the art of teasing her older brother.

Despite the occasional sibling rivalry, our family dinners are filled with laughter, affection, and the comforting sense of belonging. It's these moments - surrounded by loved ones - that remind me of what truly matters in life.As I navigate the ups and downs of teenage life in Hurricane, I've come to realize that each day brings new discoveries and opportunities for growth. Whether it's discovering a hidden talent for photography, joining the school newspaper, or simply spending time with friends, I've learned to embrace the journey with an open heart.

One day, while exploring the town's outskirts with Kyle, we stumble upon an abandoned warehouse covered in graffiti. Intrigued, we venture inside, our footsteps echoing in the empty space.

"Think there are any ghosts in here?" Kyle jokes nervously, shining his flashlight around.

I chuckle, scanning the walls adorned with vibrant murals. "Nah, just a bunch of bored teenagers looking for a thrill."

Together, we snap photos of the graffiti art, capturing the beauty of urban decay and the creativity of unknown artists. It's moments like these - spontaneous and full of wonder - that remind me of the magic hidden within the ordinary.As the sun sets on another day in Hurricane, I find myself sitting on the porch steps, gazing at the star-studded sky above. The quiet hum of crickets fills the air, a comforting soundtrack to my thoughts.

High school won't last forever, and soon I'll be faced with choices that will shape my future. But for now, I cherish the friendships I've made, the lessons I've learned, and the moments of joy that have filled my days.

I think about Kyle's infectious laughter, Sarah's artistic spirit, and the warmth of my family's love. They've taught me that life isn't just about reaching the destination - it's about savoring the journey, one day at a time.As I drift off to sleep, I think about my dreams for the future - maybe pursuing a career in photography, traveling the world, or simply finding happiness in whatever path I choose. Whatever lies ahead, I know that I'll face it with courage, determination, and the unwavering support of those who believe in me.

Tomorrow is a new day, brimming with possibilities and adventures waiting to be discovered. And as I close my eyes, I feel a sense of excitement for the journey that lies ahead - a journey filled with laughter, friendship, and the endless possibilities of teenage life in Hurricane, Utah.

A DAY IN THE LIFE OF SPRINGTRAP AND MICHAEL

In the dimly lit workshop of Afton Robotics, Springtrap—known to his friends as William Afton—busied himself with the latest modifications to the animatronics. His mechanical creations danced under his skilled hands, each wire and circuit carefully placed to bring life to the metal and plastic.

Meanwhile, Michael Afton, his mischievous son, leaned against the doorway with a smirk on his face. He had a knack for finding trouble wherever he went, and today seemed to be no exception.

"Hey, Dad," Michael chimed in, his voice carrying a hint of mischief.

William glanced up from his workbench, a small smile quirking the corner of his lips. "What is it, Michael? Planning another prank?"

Michael feigned innocence, though the twinkle in his eye betrayed him. "Who, me? Just wondering when you're going to let me try out those new animatronics."

William chuckled, setting down his tools to give his son a playful look. "You know those are for the diner. Besides, you're still grounded from the last time you tried to sneak into Freddy's."

Michael rolled his eyes dramatically, a mock expression of disappointment on his face. "Aw, come on, Dad. Can't blame a guy for trying to impress his friends."

"You'll have your chance," William assured him, ruffling Michael's hair affectionately. "But for now, let's focus on getting these animatronics ready for their big debut."

As they worked side by side, laughter echoed through the workshop. Michael would occasionally sneak a rubber spider into his father's toolbox, only to burst into laughter when William discovered it with a theatrical gasp.

Their banter continued throughout the day, punctuated by the clatter of tools and the hum of machinery. William shared stories of his own misadventures as a child, each tale more outrageous than the last, while Michael listened with rapt attention, hanging on every word.

By evening, the workshop was alive with the warmth of their bond. They shared a pizza—Michael's favorite—among the animatronics and prototypes, swapping jokes and debating the finer points of animatronic design.

As the sun dipped below the horizon, casting long shadows across the workshop, William looked at his son with pride. "You know, Michael," he began, his voice tinged with nostalgia, "someday, all of this will be yours."

Michael grinned, his eyes sparkling with excitement. "Even the haunted robots?"

William chuckled, shaking his head fondly. "Especially the haunted robots."

And so, in the quiet moments before tragedy struck, Springtrap (William Afton) and Michael Afton shared a day filled with laughter, mischief, and a bond that transcended even the darkest shadows of Afton Robotics.

In this story, we glimpse a lighter side of William Afton and Michael Afton before the events that led to their tragic fate, showcasing their familial bond and playful dynamic amidst the world of animatronics and mischief.

THE DAY THEY BECAME FRIENDS

In a small town nestled amidst rolling hills and whispering forests, five children crossed paths one fateful summer day. Each with their own hopes and dreams, they found themselves drawn together by a shared sense of curiosity and adventure.

Cassidy was a spirited boy with bright blonde hair that shimmered like spun gold in the sunlight. He was known for his infectious laughter and boundless energy, always the first to suggest an adventure in the woods or a game of hide-and-seek.

Jeremy, a bit older than the rest, had a mischicvous glint in his eye that mirrored his father's. He was quick-witted and fearless, often leading the group into daring escapades and daring his friends to explore abandoned places.

Susie was a gentle soul with a love for animals and a knack for calming her friends' fears with a soft word or a gentle touch. She had a collection of wildflowers she'd picked from secret meadows, and she loved to weave them into garlands for her friends.

Fritz, the quietest of the group, had a keen interest in mechanics and often amazed his friends with handmade gadgets and toys. His serious demeanor hid a heart of gold, and he was always there to lend a helping hand or a listening ear.

Gabriel was the storyteller of the group, his vivid imagination spinning tales of knights and dragons that captured his friends' imaginations. He had a knack for making even the most ordinary day feel like an epic adventure.

On that summer day, fate intervened as they converged near the old playground on the outskirts of town. The sun was warm, casting dappled shadows through the leaves as they laughed and played, their voices mingling with the song of birds and the rustle of the wind.

"Let's explore the old abandoned house!" Jeremy declared suddenly, pointing towards a weathered building at the edge of the forest.

Cassidy grinned, his eyes lighting up with excitement. "Are you sure it's safe?" he asked, glancing nervously at the overgrown path leading to the house.

Jeremy shrugged, a daring smile on his face. "Only one way to find out!"

With a mixture of trepidation and excitement, the group followed Jeremy through the dense underbrush until they stood before the imposing structure. Windows were boarded up, and ivy crawled across its crumbling walls, but curiosity got the better of them.

As they ventured inside, their footsteps echoed in the empty rooms, the air thick with the scent of dust and decay. Fritz marveled at the remnants of machinery scattered about, while Susie picked her way delicately through the debris, her eyes wide with wonder.

Gabriel, ever the storyteller, spun tales of the house's mysterious past—ghosts that roamed the halls and treasures hidden in forgotten rooms. His words sparked both fear and fascination among his friends, drawing them closer together in the face of the unknown.

Hours passed in a blur as they explored every corner of the house, their laughter and whispers echoing through the empty halls. They discovered hidden passages and secret rooms, their hearts racing with excitement at each new discovery.

At sunset, they gathered in the overgrown garden behind the house, their faces flushed with excitement and their minds buzzing with tales of their adventure. They sat in a circle, hands clasped together, and made a pact of friendship that would bind them together forever.

"We'll always be there for each other, no matter what," Jeremy declared solemnly, his gaze sweeping over his friends.

"And we'll never forget this day," Cassidy added, his voice filled with a sense of wonder.

The others nodded in agreement, their bond forged in the crucible of shared adventure and discovery. As the stars began to twinkle in the evening sky, they knew that their lives had been forever changed by the magic of that summer day.

Little did they know that their friendship would face a tragic and mysterious fate, intertwining their lives in ways they could never have imagined. But for now, in the glow of friendship and the promise of endless summers ahead, they reveled in the joy of being young and free, their hearts filled with hope and the promise of tomorrow.

THE GREAT fAZBEAR PIZZA PARTY

Freddy Fazbear's Pizza had always been a magical place where children's laughter filled the air, and families came together for fun and festivities. But there was one day each year that stood out above all others: The Great Fazbear Pizza Party. It was a day of unlimited pizza, games, and surprises, and this year promised to be the best yet.

It was a sunny morning in June when the announcement was made. Freddy Fazbear, the cheerful and charismatic leader of the animatronics, stepped onto the stage, microphone in hand. The restaurant was packed with excited children and their parents, all waiting to hear the news.

"Ladies and gentlemen, boys and girls," Freddy began with his trademark grin, "it's that time of year again! The Great Fazbear Pizza Party is just around the corner! This year, we have more games, more prizes, and more pizza than ever before!"

The crowd erupted in cheers and applause. Chica, the bubbly chicken animatronic, and Bonnie, the fun-loving bunny, joined Freddy on stage, waving to the audience. Foxy, the adventurous pirate fox, peeked out from behind the curtain, giving a mischievous wink.The following days were a whirlwind of activity. The animatronics worked tirelessly to prepare for the big day. Freddy supervised the decoration of the main dining hall, ensuring that every banner and balloon was perfectly placed. Chica was in charge of the kitchen, baking tray after tray of delicious pizzas with all sorts of toppings.

Bonnie, with his knack for creativity, set up a series of fun games and activities, from ring tosses to balloon dart games. Foxy, always the performer, rehearsed a special pirate show that he promised would be the highlight of the party.

The night before the party, the animatronics gathered in the main hall, admiring their hard work. "It's going to be amazing!" Chica said, her eyes sparkling with excitement.

"Aye, it'll be a day to remember," Foxy agreed, giving his hook a dramatic flourish.The sun rose on the day of The Great Fazbear Pizza Party, and the restaurant was buzzing with anticipation. Families began to arrive, greeted by the cheerful animatronics. The air was filled with the scent of fresh pizza and the sound of joyful laughter.

Freddy welcomed everyone at the entrance, shaking hands and posing for photos. "Welcome to the best party of the year!" he exclaimed, his voice full of enthusiasm.

Inside, the dining hall was a riot of color and excitement. Children ran from game to game, collecting tickets to trade for prizes. Chica's kitchen was a hive of activity, with pizzas flying out of the oven faster than they could be served.One of the most popular attractions was Bonnie's Balloon Dart Game. Children lined up to take their shot, aiming carefully at the colorful balloons. Bonnie cheered them on, his guitar slung over his shoulder. "You can do it!" he encouraged, clapping as each balloon popped.

Nearby, Chica hosted a pizza-eating contest. The contestants, both kids and adults, dug into their slices with gusto, trying to eat as much as they could in the time limit. Chica laughed and cheered them on, occasionally sneaking a slice for herself.

Foxy's Pirate Cove was a huge hit. He performed daring sword tricks and told tales of buried treasure, his audience hanging on his every word. "Arr, mateys! Who's ready to find some treasure?" he called out, leading a group of excited children on a treasure hunt around the restaurant.As the afternoon turned into evening, Freddy gathered everyone for a special surprise. "Ladies and gentlemen, gather round! It's time for our very special magic show!" he announced.

The lights dimmed, and the crowd hushed in anticipation. The stage curtains parted to reveal a magician in a sparkling costume. "Hello, everyone! I'm Magic Mike, and I'm here to dazzle you with tricks and illusions!" he declared.

The show was a mesmerizing display of magic. Mike pulled rabbits out of hats, made objects disappear and reappear, and even performed a daring escape trick. But the highlight of the show was when he invited Freddy, Chica, Bonnie, and Foxy onto the stage.

"Let's see if our friends here have a little magic of their own," Mike said with a wink. He handed Freddy a deck of cards, and to everyone's amazement, Freddy performed a flawless card trick, revealing the chosen card to loud applause.

Chica levitated a pizza box, much to the delight of the audience, while Bonnie played a song on his guitar that made flowers bloom on stage. Foxy, ever the showman, produced a shower of golden coins from his treasure chest, tossing them into the crowd.As the sun began to set, Freddy called everyone back to the main hall for the grand finale. "Thank you all for making this day so special," he said. "We have one last surprise for you."

The lights dimmed, and the animatronics took their places on stage. The music started, and they launched into a lively performance, singing and dancing to the theme of Freddy Fazbear's Pizza. The crowd clapped and sang along, the energy in the room electric.

As the final notes of the song faded, fireworks erupted outside, lighting up the night sky. The children oohed and aahed, their faces glowing with happiness.With the fireworks display over, families began to make their way home, tired but happy. Freddy, Chica, Bonnie, and Foxy stood at the entrance, waving goodbye and thanking everyone for coming.

"That was the best party ever!" one little girl exclaimed, clutching a plush Freddy bear she had won.

"Can't wait for next year!" another child called out, high-fiving Bonnie.

As the last guests left, the animatronics gathered in the now-quiet dining hall, looking around at the remnants of the day's festivities. "We did it," Freddy said, a note of pride in his voice. "We made so many people happy."

Chica nodded, "It was a lot of work, but seeing those smiles made it all worth it."

Bonnie and Foxy agreed, both feeling a sense of accomplishment. They had come together as a team, each contributing their unique talents to create a day filled with joy and laughter.As they cleaned up, the animatronics reflected on the day. "You know," Bonnie said, stacking chairs, "I think this was our best party yet."

"Aye," Foxy agreed, sweeping up confetti. "But I've got some ideas for next year. How about a pirate ship ride?"

Chica laughed, "And maybe a pizza-making contest where everyone can create their own unique pizza."

Freddy smiled, "Those are great ideas. We'll make next year's party even better."

With the cleanup done, the animatronics gathered in the main hall one last time. Freddy looked around at his friends, feeling a deep sense of gratitude. "Thank you, everyone. We couldn't have done it without each other."

They shared a group hug, their hearts full of happiness and anticipation for the future.As the lights dimmed and the animatronics settled into their charging stations, the restaurant grew quiet. The echoes of laughter and music still lingered in the air, a reminder of the wonderful day they had shared.

Freddy looked out at the darkened hall, already planning for the next Great Fazbear Pizza Party. "Goodnight, everyone," he whispered. "Until tomorrow, when the fun begins again."

Chica, Bonnie, and Foxy drifted into standby mode, their systems humming softly as they dreamed of new adventures and happy faces.The Great Fazbear Pizza Party had been a day of joy, laughter, and unforgettable memories. But it was more than just a single event; it was a promise. A promise that no matter what, Freddy Fazbear's Pizza would always be a place where dreams came true and happiness reigned.

As the sun rose on a new day, the animatronics powered up, ready to welcome a new group of visitors. The magic of Freddy Fazbear's Pizza was alive and well, and the adventures were far from over.

Freddy stepped onto the stage, microphone in hand, and greeted the new arrivals with his signature smile. "Welcome to Freddy Fazbear's Pizza, where the fun never ends!"

And so, with hearts full of joy and minds brimming with ideas, the animatronics embarked on another day of fun, knowing that every moment spent bringing smiles to their guests was a moment well spent.

The Great Fazbear Pizza Party was just one chapter in their story, but it was a chapter that would be remembered for years to come. And as long as there were children to laugh and play, the magic of Freddy Fazbear's Pizza would never fade.

THE SURPRISE BIRTHDAY BASH AT FREDDY FAZBEAR'S PIZZA

It was a sunny Saturday afternoon, and Freddy Fazbear's Pizza was buzzing with excitement. The animatronics were polished to perfection, their gears humming with anticipation for the special event about to unfold. Today was Gabriel's birthday, and his parents had planned the ultimate surprise bash at his favorite place in town—Freddy Fazbear's Pizza.

Gabriel, a bubbly seven-year-old with a penchant for adventure, had no idea what awaited him as he walked through the doors of the pizzeria. His eyes widened in awe at the sight of Freddy, Bonnie, and Chica, standing tall on the stage, ready to perform. The colorful balloons and decorations adorned every corner, creating a festive atmosphere that filled the air with joy.

As Gabriel explored the arcade games with his friends, Freddy Fazbear himself approached, his voice booming cheerfully through the speakers. "Hey there, birthday star! Ready for some fun?" Gabriel grinned from ear to ear, nodding enthusiastically as Freddy led him to the prize counter. With a wave of his paw, Freddy presented Gabriel with a special birthday hat and a stack of tokens for the games.

Meanwhile, in the kitchen, Bonnie and Chica were busy preparing Gabriel's favorite pizza—extra cheese and pepperoni, just the way he liked it. They giggled and exchanged playful banter as they worked, eager to surprise Gabriel with their culinary skills.

As the afternoon rolled on, Gabriel and his friends took turns playing games, winning tickets, and exchanging them for prizes. Bonnie and Chica joined in, showcasing their dance moves and singing along to Gabriel's favorite songs. Laughter echoed through the pizzeria as the children enjoyed the interactive show and the animatronics' antics.

When it was time for cake, everyone gathered around a table adorned with candles and a massive chocolate cake topped with Freddy,

Bonnie, and Chica figurines. Gabriel's eyes lit up with delight as his parents brought out the cake, and the animatronics led the room in a lively rendition of "Happy Birthday."

After blowing out the candles and making a wish, Gabriel thanked Freddy, Bonnie, and Chica for the best birthday ever. "You're welcome, buddy!" Freddy boomed with a wink. "Remember, every day is a celebration here at Freddy Fazbear's Pizza!"

As the evening drew to a close, Gabriel hugged his friends and bid farewell to his beloved animatronic pals, promising to return soon for more adventures. With hearts full of joy and memories to cherish, Gabriel and his family left Freddy Fazbear's Pizza, already planning their next visit to the place where dreams come true and happiness is always on the menu.

A DAY OF WHIMSY WITH THE AFTOM FAMILY

In a cozy town nestled between rolling hills and whispering forests, lived the Afton family—William, his wife Clara, and their three children: Michael, Elizabeth, and little Evan. The Aftons were known for their creativity and love for adventure, which often led them on whimsical journeys through their vibrant imagination.

One sunny Friday morning, William, a skilled inventor, surprised his family with a magical contraption he had been secretly working on—a fantastical time-traveling carousel. Built in their backyard, the carousel shimmered with colors of the rainbow and emitted a soft, enchanting hum.

"Step right up, my dear family!" William exclaimed, his eyes twinkling with excitement. "Today, we embark on an adventure through time and space!"

Michael, a daring young boy with a fascination for dinosaurs, eagerly climbed aboard the carousel first. "I want to go to the Jurassic period!" he declared, clutching his toy dinosaur tightly.

Elizabeth, a sweet and imaginative girl with a love for fairy tales, followed next. "I wish to visit a magical kingdom with unicorns and dragons!" she chimed in, her eyes sparkling with anticipation.

Little Evan, their youngest and full of boundless energy, bounced on his toes. "I want to see pirates!" he exclaimed with a big grin.

Clara, a kind-hearted soul with a passion for history, smiled warmly as she took William's hand. "Surprise us, dear," she said playfully. "Where shall we venture first?"

With a flick of William's wrist and a burst of colorful sparks, the carousel whirred to life, spinning faster and faster until the Afton family found themselves transported to their first destination—a bustling medieval market.

The air was filled with the aroma of freshly baked bread and the lively chatter of merchants selling their wares. Knights in shining armor trotted past on majestic steeds, while jesters entertained crowds with juggling acts and acrobatics. Elizabeth gasped in delight as she spotted a real-life unicorn grazing in a nearby meadow, its horn glinting in the sunlight.

Next, they traveled to ancient Egypt, where towering pyramids loomed against a backdrop of endless desert sands. Michael marveled at the intricate hieroglyphs etched into stone walls, imagining himself as an intrepid explorer uncovering ancient secrets. Elizabeth danced gleefully with Cleopatra herself, adorned in shimmering jewels and elegant robes.

Their adventures continued as they journeyed to the golden age of piracy, sailing aboard a grand galleon through stormy seas and hidden coves. Michael and Elizabeth donned pirate hats and swashbuckling attire, joining a crew of mischievous buccaneers in search of buried treasure. Little Evan, with a spyglass in hand, eagerly scanned the horizon for adventure.

With each twist of the carousel's magical gears, the Afton family visited new realms and encountered fantastical creatures. They frolicked with friendly dragons in enchanted forests, soared through the cosmos aboard shimmering starships, and even danced with dinosaurs beneath a canopy of prehistoric ferns.

As the sun began to set, casting a warm glow over the horizon, the carousel gently brought the Afton family back to their backyard. They disembarked with hearts full of laughter and minds buzzing with tales of their extraordinary journey.

Clara hugged William tightly, her eyes shimmering with gratitude. "Thank you, my love, for such a magical day," she whispered, her voice filled with warmth.

Michael, Elizabeth, and Evan clamored for one more ride on the carousel, already dreaming of their next adventure. William chuckled and winked at Clara, knowing that their family's bond grew stronger with each whimsical journey through time and space.

And so, in their cozy town nestled between rolling hills and whispering forests, the Afton family continued to embrace the joy of imagination, forever bound by love, laughter, and the enchanting carousel that made dreams come alive.

A DAY OF ADVENTURE AT FREDDY FAZBEAR'S MEGA PIZZAPLEX

It was an exciting day at Freddy Fazbear's Mega PizzaPlex, the largest and most technologically advanced entertainment complex in town. The sun shone brightly outside as families lined up eagerly to experience a day of fun and wonder. Among them was Jeremy, a curious and adventurous ten-year-old who couldn't wait to explore every corner of the Mega PizzaPlex.

Accompanied by his older brother Michael and his little sister Elizabeth, Jeremy entered the Mega PizzaPlex with wide eyes, marveling at the towering animatronic statues and the colorful displays that welcomed them. Today was a special occasion—Jeremy's birthday—and his parents had surprised him with tickets to explore all the attractions and rides.

As they walked through the bustling corridors, Jeremy couldn't contain his excitement. Animatronic characters greeted them with cheerful waves and high-fives, their LED screens displaying welcoming messages. "Happy birthday, Jeremy!" Freddy Fazbear's cheerful voice echoed through the air, making Jeremy beam with delight.

Their first stop was Glamrock Freddy's Dance Party, where Jeremy, Michael, and Elizabeth joined other children in a lively dance-off. The animatronics, led by Glamrock Freddy himself, showed off their best moves, encouraging everyone to dance along to catchy tunes. Jeremy and Michael laughed as they spun and jumped to the music, earning cheers and applause from the audience.

Next, they ventured into Roxanne Wolf's Laser Tag Arena, where they suited up in neon vests and armed themselves with glowing blasters. Jeremy and Michael teamed up against Elizabeth and a group of new friends they met at the Mega PizzaPlex. They dashed through neon-lit corridors, dodging lasers and tagging opponents with precision. Jeremy couldn't stop grinning as they emerged victorious in a blaze of colorful lights.

After a thrilling round of laser tag, they explored Monty's Gator Golf, an indoor mini-golf course with challenging holes themed around the Mega PizzaPlex's animatronic characters. Jeremy and Michael navigated through obstacles and tricky slopes, cheering each other on with every successful putt. Elizabeth, too young to play, giggled as she watched her brothers compete.

As lunchtime approached, they visited Chica's Party World, a vibrant dining area filled with tables adorned with balloons and party hats. Chica herself emerged from the kitchen, carrying trays of pizzas topped with Jeremy's favorite toppings—pepperoni, mushrooms, and extra cheese. Jeremy, Michael, and Elizabeth devoured their slices between bouts of laughter and conversation about their favorite attractions so far.

After lunch, they ventured into Freddy Fazbear's Maze of Mirrors, where twisting corridors and cleverly placed mirrors created an illusion of endless paths. Jeremy and Michael navigated the maze, laughing as they bumped into mirrored walls and occasionally found themselves face-to-face with their own reflections. Elizabeth giggled from the sidelines, cheering them on with each twist and turn.

As the day drew to a close, Jeremy and his family gathered in the main plaza for the grand finale—a spectacular fireworks display launched from the top of the Mega PizzaPlex. Colorful explosions illuminated the night sky, reflecting in the eyes of children and adults alike. Jeremy hugged his family tightly, feeling grateful for the unforgettable birthday adventure they had shared.

As they left Freddy Fazbear's Mega PizzaPlex, Jeremy turned to his parents with a wide grin. "Thank you for the best birthday ever!" he exclaimed, his heart filled with happiness and excitement. For Jeremy, and for every family who visited the Mega PizzaPlex, it was more than just an entertainment complex—it was a place where dreams came true, laughter echoed through the halls, and memories were made in the magical world of animatronic wonders.

A MAGICAL CHRISTMAS AT FREDDY FAZBEAR'S PIZZA

In the heart of a bustling town adorned with twinkling lights and festive decorations, Freddy Fazbear's Pizza stood as a beacon of joy and wonderment. Inside the beloved pizzeria, where animatronic characters came to life and laughter filled the air, preparations were underway for a magical Christmas celebration unlike any other.It was a snowy December morning, and the Afton and Emily families arrived at Freddy Fazbear's Pizza with hearts full of anticipation. William Afton and Henry Emily, the owners and creative minds behind the pizzeria, had spared no expense in transforming the venue into a winter wonderland.

The dining area sparkled with Christmas lights and garlands, and a towering tree adorned with colorful ornaments and twinkling lights stood proudly in the center. Tables were adorned with festive tablecloths and candles, creating a warm and inviting atmosphere for the guests.

"Wow, Dad, look at all the decorations!" exclaimed Michael Afton, his eyes widening with delight as he took in the festive scene.

William chuckled, ruffling Michael's hair affectionately. "It's Christmas, son. We wanted to make it special for everyone."Inside the pizzeria, families gathered around tables, sharing stories and laughter as they enjoyed slices of Freddy's famous pizza and sipped on hot cocoa. Children dashed about, their cheeks flushed with excitement as they interacted with the animatronic characters – Freddy, Bonnie, Chica, and Foxy – who roamed the dining area, singing Christmas carols and spreading holiday cheer.

Elizabeth Afton and Charlie Emily, inseparable friends since childhood, giggled as they danced with Chica and Bonnie, their voices blending with the cheerful melodies echoing through the pizzeria.

"Isn't this the best Christmas ever?" Charlie exclaimed, twirling in sync with Chica.

Elizabeth nodded enthusiastically. "Absolutely! I love seeing everyone so happy."As the afternoon progressed, Mr. Scott, the manager of Freddy Fazbear's Pizza, announced a series of festive activities for the guests to enjoy. In the arcade area, children and adults alike competed in friendly games of snowball toss and pin the nose on Rudolph, with plush toys and Freddy Fazbear merchandise as prizes.

William and Henry joined in the fun, showcasing their skills in the snowball toss and challenging each other to see who could score the most points.

"Looks like I win this round, Henry!" William teased, giving his friend a playful nudge.

Henry laughed good-naturedly. "You got lucky, old friend. Let's see how you do in the next game!"In a cozy corner of the pizzeria, a makeshift workshop had been set up with tables stocked with colored paper, markers, and glitter. Children eagerly wrote letters to Santa Claus, sharing their Christmas wishes and dreams for the holiday season.

Evan Afton, his brow furrowed in concentration, carefully wrote his letter to Santa, asking for a new set of art supplies and a special treat for Freddy, his beloved golden retriever.

"Dear Santa," Evan wrote, his handwriting neat and deliberate. "This year, I've been really good. Please bring me some paints and a bone for Freddy. Thank you!"

Clara Afton smiled warmly, observing her youngest son's heartfelt letter. "That's a wonderful letter, Evan. Santa will be so happy to read it."

Nearby, Cassidy, Jeremy, Suzie, Gabriel, and Fritz huddled together, sharing markers and exchanging ideas for their letters to Santa. Cassidy asked for a new sketchbook, Jeremy wished for a remote-controlled car, Suzie hoped for a collection of fairy tale books, Gabriel wanted a soccer ball, and Fritz desired a telescope to explore the night sky.As the sun began to set and the pizzeria glowed with the warm light of Christmas candles, Mr. Scott gathered everyone around the main stage for a special Christmas Eve performance. The animatronic characters – Freddy,

Bonnie, Chica, and Foxy – took center stage, their voices harmonizing in a medley of classic Christmas carols that filled the room with joy and nostalgia.

Children and adults alike clapped and sang along, their spirits lifted by the magical atmosphere and the timeless melodies that echoed through the pizzeria.

"Merry Christmas, everyone!" Mr. Scott announced, his voice filled with joy. "Thank you for joining us in celebrating this special day."As the performance drew to a close, the Afton and Emily families gathered around a long table in the dining area, where a festive feast awaited them. The table groaned under the weight of roasted turkey, mashed potatoes, cranberry sauce, and an array of mouthwatering desserts – from pumpkin pie to sugar cookies decorated with colorful icing.

"This looks amazing, Mom," Michael remarked, taking a seat beside Clara.

Clara beamed with pride. "Thank you, Michael. I wanted to make sure we had all your favorite dishes."

Around the table, laughter and conversation flowed freely as the families shared stories, exchanged gifts, and toasted to the joyous occasion. William and Henry raised their glasses in a toast to friendship, family, and the spirit of Christmas that brought them all together.As the evening drew to a close, each child received a special gift – a plush toy of their favorite animatronic character, lovingly wrapped in festive paper and tied with a ribbon. Evan hugged his plush Freddy bear tightly, his eyes shining with happiness as he thanked his parents.

"Thank you, Mom, Dad," Evan whispered, his voice filled with gratitude.

Clara kissed his cheek gently. "You're welcome, sweetheart. Merry Christmas."

Outside, snowflakes danced in the air, transforming the pizzeria's parking lot into a winter wonderland. Families bid farewell with hugs and promises to meet again soon, their hearts full of cherished memories and the magic of Christmas at Freddy Fazbear's Pizza.

FAREWELL

As we turn the final page of "Tales from Fazbear's," I want to extend my heartfelt thanks to you, dear reader, for joining me on this delightful journey. We've explored the charming and whimsical world of Freddy Fazbear's Pizza, where every story brought a smile, a laugh, and a touch of magic.

Throughout these tales, we've celebrated the joy of friendship, the excitement of discovery, and the simple pleasures of fun-filled days at Freddy's. Your imagination and enthusiasm have made this adventure special, bringing each story to life in wonderful ways.

As we say goodbye, let's hold on to the happiness and wonder that Freddy Fazbear's Pizza brings. Remember the delightful characters, the cheerful moments, and the boundless fun that make this place so magical. Even though our journey in this book has come to an end, the spirit of Fazbear's lives on in our hearts.

Though these tales may be complete, the joy and laughter they inspire continue. Perhaps new stories will emerge, inviting us back to the enchanting world of Freddy Fazbear's Pizza. Until then, let's keep the fun and joy alive in our own lives, cherishing the memories we've made.

Thank you for being a part of "Tales from Fazbear's." Farewell for now, but remember, the magic of Freddy's is always with us as long as we keep smiling and dreaming.

Until we meet again, stay joyful, keep dreaming, and may the adventures continue in your heart.

Farewell, and happy memories!